W9-DIL-226

Parent's Introduction

We Both Read is the first series of books designed to invite parents and children to share the reading of a story by taking turns reading aloud. This "shared reading" innovation, which was developed in conjunction with early reading specialists, invites parents to read the more sophisticated text on the left-hand pages, while children are encouraged to read the right-hand pages, which have been written at one of three early reading levels.

Reading aloud is one of the most important activities parents can share with their child to assist their reading development. However, *We Both Read* goes beyond reading *to* a child and allows parents to share reading *with* a child. *We Both Read* is so powerful and effective because it combines two key elements in learning: "showing" (the parent reads) and "doing" (the child reads). The result is not only faster reading development for the child, but a much more enjoyable and enriching experience for both!

Most of the words used in the child's text should be familiar to them. Others can easily be sounded out. An occasional difficult word will be first introduced in the parent's text, distinguished with **bold lettering**. Pointing out these words, as you read them, will help familiarize them to your child. You may also find it helpful to read the entire book aloud yourself the first time, then invite your child to participate on the second reading. Also note that the parent's text is preceded by a "talking parent" icon: ; and the child's text is preceded by a "talking child" icon: .

We Both Read books is a fun, easy way to encourage and help your child to read — and a wonderful way to start your child off on a lifetime of reading enjoyment!

We Both Read: Ben and Becky in the Haunted House

––––––––––––––––––––––––––––––

Text Copyright © 1999 by Sindy McKay
Illustrations Copyright © 1999 by Meredith Johnson
All rights reserved

We Both Read® is a trademark of Treasure Bay, Inc.

Published by Treasure Bay, Inc.
17 Parkgrove Drive
South San Francisco, CA 94080 USA

PRINTED IN SINGAPORE

Library of Congress Catalog Card Number: 98-61766

Hardcover ISBN 1-891327-14-3
Paperback ISBN 1-891327-18-6

FIRST EDITION

We Both Read® Books
Patent No. 5,957,693

Visit us online at:
www.webothread.com

WE BOTH READ™

Ben & Becky in the Haunted House

By Sindy McKay
Illustrated by Meredith Johnson

TREASURE BAY

My name is Ben and I believe in **ghosts**. I also believe in phantoms, poltergeists, spirits and all things haunted and spooky. I think that stuff is very cool. So does my **Grandpa**.

My big sister Becky (who thinks she's real smart) used to say that believing in ghosts was ridiculous. She used to say that ghosts are merely a figment of an overactive imagination. (Becky loves using big words like that.)

That's what Becky *used* to say about **ghosts**. But that's not what she says *now*. Not after what happened at my **Grandpa's** house last week.

Let me tell you all about it.

Last week we visited my grandparents.

Grandpa is like me — he **believes** in ghosts. Grandma is like Becky and she thinks that Grandpa behaves like a big kid sometimes. (Which he does, and that is why I like him so much!)

Grandpa said, "What about that old house Frank Jones owns up the street, Ethel? That place is **haunted** as sure as I'm sitting here."

I couldn't **believe** my ears. There was a **haunted** house up the street? This was too cool to be true!

I asked Grandpa if we could see it. He said yes. He asked Becky to come too. She said she had nothing better to do.

The big old house looked pretty spooky, even in broad daylight. The front gate, hanging from one hinge, creaked and banged in the breeze.

Suddenly Grandpa's dog, Sparky, bristled and **growled** deep in his throat. Grandpa spoke in a **whisper.**

"Do you feel it, kids? Do you feel the presence of a ghostly apparition?"

"Yes, I feel it," I **whispered** back to Grandpa.

Sparky **growled** a little louder.

"Well, I don't feel a thing," said Becky.

Grandpa said she'd feel it if she were here at night. And that gave Grandpa a very cool idea.

I **thought Grandma's** eyes were going to pop out of her head when Grandpa told her his very cool idea.

"You want to spend a whole night in that drafty old dilapidated Jones house?" she cried.

Grandpa nodded. "Spoke with Frank Jones about it this afternoon. It's okay with him if it's okay with you."

Grandma sighed. "Well, I suppose you better pack some appropriate **equipment** then."

Grandma said we would need sleeping bags. Grandpa **thought** we needed a flashlight.

I wanted to bring ghost-busting **equipment.** But Grandpa said that stuff was only in the movies. This was real life. And this was a real ghost.

That night we trudged up the street to the old Jones house. It looked even spookier at night than it did during the day.

A light rain started to fall as Grandpa opened the creaking gate and we stepped into the yard. Leaves crunched underfoot as we walked toward the **huge** wooden front door.

Grandpa **wondered** if the leaves crunched when the ghost walked on them too.

At last we reached the **huge** front door. I **wondered** who was going to open it. Becky said Grandpa should do it. Grandpa said Becky should do it.

Then the huge front door opened all by itself.

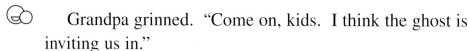

Grandpa grinned. "Come on, kids. I think the ghost is inviting us in."

Sparky ran inside, barking courageously at the **cobwebs** in the hallway. Grandpa and I followed eagerly behind.

Becky didn't want to come in. I could tell. But instead of saying so, she just repeated what she had already said about a million times that day—"There's no such thing as ghosts!"

Becky stepped inside. Then the big door slammed shut behind her.

Grandpa led Becky and me through the house. It was full of dust and **cobwebs.** He led us to the living room. We couldn't believe what we saw.

The room was spotless. A **cozy** fire roared in the fireplace and a **delicious** picnic was spread out on the floor.

"Wow," I whispered, "this is really eerie."

Grandpa started munching on a fried chicken leg. "Yep. But there's no sense letting good food go to waste just 'cause it was prepared by a ghost."

We all sat down and ate. The rain began to come down hard. But we were safe and **cozy** inside. And the food was **delicious.** I asked Grandpa to tell us a story.

He told us the story of the haunted house.

"A long time ago," he began, "**Captain Benjamin** Jones and his wife Eliza lived happily in this house. But every time the Captain went to sea, Eliza went mad with loneliness. Inconsolable, she would sit at the attic window, awaiting his return. All day the servants could hear her, rocking and moaning as she called out his name, '**Beee-e-en**! **Beee-e-en**!'"

The way Grandpa said "**Beee-e-en**" gave me the creeps! But I told him to go on with his story.

"One day there was a huge storm at sea," he said. "**Captain Benjamin's** ship was lost. And so was Captain Benjamin."

"Eliza refused to believe he was never coming back. She continued to wait in the window for him every day. And when darkness fell, she would light her candelabra and wait for him through the night."

Thunder rumbled ominously as Grandpa added, "They say you can still see the lights of her candelabra up in the attic window — even though Eliza died one hundred years ago."

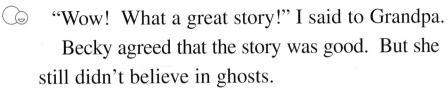 "Wow! What a great story!" I said to Grandpa.

Becky agreed that the story was good. But she still didn't believe in ghosts.

I begged him to tell us another one. But Grandpa said it was time to go to bed.

We huddled down into our sleeping bags and closed our eyes. A few minutes later, we heard a noise — criik-craak, criik-craak — like the sound of a chair rocking back and forth.

"Sounds like Eliza's in a haunting mood tonight," Grandpa whispered.

Then he rolled over and went to sleep.

I guess I finally fell asleep too because suddenly I was awakened by a clap of thunder that shook the whole house!

I wanted to be sure Grandpa was okay. So I
reached for his hand. But Grandpa was gone!
I ran to Becky and tried to wake her up.
"Becky," I yelled. "Grandpa's gone! Sparky too!"

Becky didn't even open her eyes as she muttered, "Relax, Ben. They probably just went to the bathroom."

Probably. But I decided to stay up and wait for them anyway. I waited a long time. But they didn't come back.

And then I heard a voice. It was faint and distant. But I definitely heard it. And the voice moaned . . .

"Beee-e-en! Beee-e-en!"

It was the ghost. It was Eliza!

Becky heard it too. She sat up and took my hand.

"Come on, Ben," she said. "We have to find Grandpa."

Becky led the way into the dining room and we could hardly see a thing. The batteries in our flashlight were dying and its light was beginning to **fade**.

Suddenly a flash of **lightning** lit up the place like a spotlight and Becky and I saw something over by the window. Something white and flowing.

Something like a ghost.

I jumped! Becky screamed! The light from the lightning **faded** away.

Then the **lightning** flashed again! And the room lit up again! And Becky and I saw the ghost again!

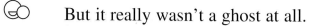 But it really wasn't a ghost at all.

"It's just an illusion," said Becky with great relief.

"It looks like a *curtain* to me," I said as I touched the torn material hanging near the window.

We continued our search for Grandpa, exploring the whole downstairs, our flashlight growing dimmer all the time. Then we began to climb the stairs to the second floor.

That's when I felt something tug on my leg. "Becky," I screamed! "Eliza is grabbing my leg!" Becky shined the flashlight at me. I thought I would see the small white hand of a ghost.

Instead I saw the small white muzzle of Grandpa's dog, Sparky, biting and tugging on my pants. I think Sparky was pretty worried about Grandpa, too.

"I'm glad Sparky's here," Becky said. "He'll be a real **asset** in our **search** for Grandpa."

Sparky wagged his tail and led the way as we continued to **climb** the stairs.

We **climbed** up to the second floor. We **searched** every room. But we still did not find Grandpa. And then our flashlight went out.

"This is quite a predicament," Becky **whispered** in the dark. "What do we do now?"

I was about to answer when we heard Sparky barking. We moved toward the sound and found him at the attic steps.

And there on a small table was a fully lit **candelabra**.

"Do you think it's Eliza's?" I **whispered**.

"I don't care if it is," said Becky. "I'm just glad it's here. Now let's go find Grandpa."

We took the **candelabra**. We climbed up the attic stairs. Becky opened the attic door and looked inside. Then Becky started to scream.

Inside the attic was Eliza! I joined Becky and together we screamed for about two whole minutes! Lightning flashed! Thunder roared! Sparky howled!

Then suddenly, through all this noise, we heard the ghastly moaning voice calling to us again! "Beee-e-en! Beee-e-ecky!"

I wanted to run away. So did Becky! But we couldn't just leave Grandpa.

Sparky ran up to Eliza, the ghost. He barked. He tugged on her dress. But Eliza didn't move at all.

Maybe it wasn't Eliza the ghost, after all.

Sparky tugged until Eliza **finally** fell over. That's when Becky and I began to laugh.

"It's just another illusion," said Becky. "She's nothing more than a dress form with an old dress and a big hat!"

We were still laughing when we heard the **moaning** again. "Beee-e-en! Beee-e-ecky!"

Sparky's ears perked up and he took off, racing toward the sound. Becky and I shouted for him to stop!

Sparky did **finally** stop. He stopped right in front
of Grandpa. And Grandpa was **moaning**.

"Be-e-en! Be-e-ecky! I'm so glad that you're here!"

Becky and I realized that all the moaning we'd heard had been Grandpa—moaning in pain!

Grandpa told us how he'd planned to give us a good, fun scare by making up the dress form to look like Eliza.

"But when I came up to the attic to get 'er," he explained, "I tripped over a loose board and hurt my **ankle** real bad. I'm afraid it might be broken."

Becky told Grandpa not to worry. She knew what to do. She told him not to move his **ankle**.

"I'll get help," she said. "Ben will stay with you."

In no time at all, help arrived and Grandpa was taken to the hospital. The doctors there told him it was just a bad sprain and that his ankle would be fine in a couple of days. They also told him to stay away from haunted houses.

When we finally got back to Grandpa's house, he told us the whole story.

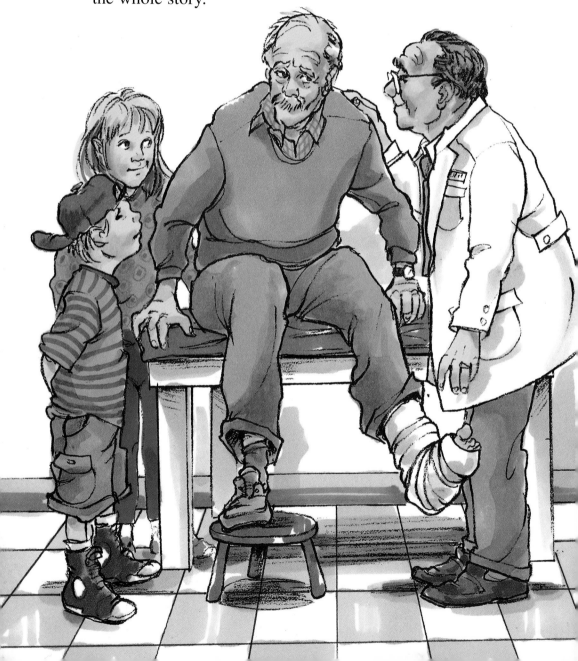

Grandpa told us he just wanted to have some fun. He asked Mr. Jones to help him. Mr. Jones lit the fire before we got there. And he made the rocking chair rock in the attic. Grandpa even talked Grandma into helping. She set up the dinner.

Then they both went home and Grandpa was on his own. "It was my job to get 'Eliza' out of the attic and down the stairs. That's when I tripped and hurt my ankle."

"Oh, I get it," I said. "Then you must be the one who lit the candelabra too."

Grandpa looked at me like I was crazy. "Candelabra? I didn't light any candelabra."

Becky and I looked at each other. Grandpa didn't light the candelabra. So who did?

"Well, Ben," said Becky, "I still don't believe in ghosts. But I'm starting to believe in Eliza."

I believe in Eliza too.

**If you liked
Ben & Becky in the Haunted House, here are two other
We Both Read™ Books you are sure to enjoy!**

Ben and Becky finally convince their parents to let them have a pet. Becky wants to get a kitten, but Ben wants to get a snake. They go with their father to pick out a pet and cause hilarious excitement when they accidentally let the pet store's snake loose in the mall!